Race Day in Rainbow Falls

ORCHARD

"Look, Twilight!" called Spike, bursting into their home with a scroll gripped in his claw. "We've got an official letter from the mayor of Ponyville!"

"Really?" cried Twilight Sparkle, taking the scroll. "Let's open it and see what it says."

ORCHARD BOOKS

First published in Great Britain in 2017 by The Watts Publishing Group

1 3 5 7 9 10 8 6 4 2

HASBRO and its logo, MY LITTLE PONY and all related characters are
trademarks of Hasbro and are used with permission.

A CIP catalogue record for this book is available from the British Library

ISBN 978 1 40835 018 8

Printed and bound in China

Orchard Books
An imprint of Hachette Children's Group
Part of The Watts Publishing Group Limited
Carmelite House
50 Victoria Embankment
London EC4Y 0DZ
An Hachette UK Company

www.hachette.co.uk
www.hachettechildrens.co.uk

Licensed by:

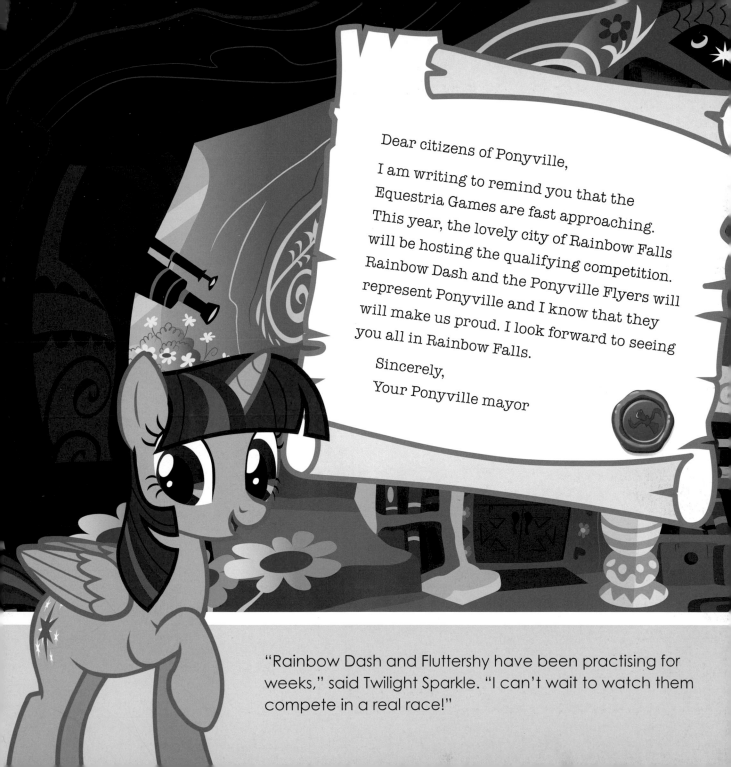

Dear citizens of Ponyville,

I am writing to remind you that the Equestria Games are fast approaching. This year, the lovely city of Rainbow Falls will be hosting the qualifying competition. Rainbow Dash and the Ponyville Flyers will represent Ponyville and I know that they will make us proud. I look forward to seeing you all in Rainbow Falls.

Sincerely,
Your Ponyville mayor

"Rainbow Dash and Fluttershy have been practising for weeks," said Twilight Sparkle. "I can't wait to watch them compete in a real race!"

Soon it was time for the ponies of Ponyville to set off for Rainbow Falls. Spike was helping Twilight to prepare for her trip. "I wish I could come with you," he sighed. "Don't forget to send me lots of postcards!"

"You have a very important job to do here," Twilight reminded him. "Looking after Ponyville's animals. We're all relying on you, Spike!"

"I'll be the best critter-sitter ever!" promised Spike.

Giving the little dragon one last hug, Twilight set off. "I'll miss you," she called. "See you in a few days!"

At the station, Twilight and her friends stepped aboard the Friendship Express. "I wonder what Rainbow Falls will be like," said Fluttershy nervously. "Do you think it's big and scary?"

"Hardly! There are sparkling rainbows everywhere," said Applejack.

"I can't wait to compete in the games!" cried Rainbow Dash. "This is the most exciting thing that's ever happened to me!"

"Me too!" agreed the other ponies. "We can't wait to watch you compete."

Pinkie Pie was already wearing her cheerleading outfit. "I'm going to make so much noise!" she yelled.

"Please wait till you get to Rainbow Falls!" laughed Rarity.

It wasn't long before the train approached Rainbow Falls. The view was breathtaking. "What an amazing place!" exclaimed Rainbow Dash.

"It says in my guidebook that the town was built next to a waterfall," Twilight Sparkle told her friends.

"This pony hasn't got time for guidebooks," Rainbow Dash said as they stepped off the train. "Fluttershy and I are going straight to the arena to practice for the flying competition!"

Dear Spike,

Rainbow Falls is just as pretty as we all imagined!
There are rainbows everywhere - and not just in the
sky. The ponies are very excited to be hosting the
qualifying competition for the Equestria Games.
Rainbow Dash and Fluttershy are practising right now,
but I stayed in the hotel to write to you! I hope you are
having fun back in Ponyville.

XOXO, Twilight Sparkle

After writing to Spike, Twilight Sparkle decided to explore Rainbow Falls. She began to read from her trusty guidebook:

"The Rainbow River, which runs all the way through Rainbow Falls, is one of the longest rivers in Equestria—"

THUMP!

Twilight was so busy reading her book that she bumped headlong into two ponies. "Ouch!" cried a familiar voice.

It was Pinkie Pie and Rarity! "I didn't expect to BUMP into you two," said Twilight, hugging her friends. "I'm sorry! I need to be more careful!"

Dear Spike,
I had a great day walking around Rainbow Falls with Pinkie Pie and Rarity. The town is so beautiful. The Rainbow River runs all the way through it, and there are wooden bridges to walk across and benches to sit on – perfect for reading my guidebook! I hope you're getting on well with the animals. Miss you!

Your friend, Twilight

The next day, while Rainbow Dash and Fluttershy headed off to the training ground, Twilight Sparkle, Rarity and Pinkie Pie went back to the marketplace.

"I've been wanting to get some sweets ever since yesterday," said Pinkie Pie excitedly. "Do you want some, Twilight?"

But Twilight still had her nose stuck in her guidebook. "It says here that the marketplace is . . . Hang on, ponies, are you listening?"

In fact, Rarity and Pinkie Pie had spotted something far more interesting!

A familiar figure was standing beside a wagon full of delicious-smelling cakes. "Get your apple brown Bettys here!" cried Applejack. "It's a Sweet Apple Acres family recipe!"

Soon Applejack was surrounded by a crowd of ponies eager to try her tasty Ponyville treats. Even Rainbow Dash and her flying team had made time for a snack!

Dear Spike,

Today we spent the day in the Rainbow Falls marketplace. This is where all the Rainbow Falls ponies come to set up their carts and wagons and sell things. Ponies were selling rainbow ribbons with medals on them, rainbow glasses, rainbow flags, rainbow foam hooves and unicorn horns — all in honour of the Equestria Games qualifying competition. Applejack even joined in! She set up her wagon and sold apple brown Bettys. The ponies of Rainbow Falls loved them!

Keep up the good work with the animals, and I'll write again soon.

Lots of love,
Twilight

Over at the flying arena, Rainbow Dash was putting her team through their paces. "Let's try that manoeuvre again!" she yelled to her teammates, Fluttershy and Bulk Biceps. "And try not to drop the horseshoe this time or we'll never beat the Wonderbolts!"

Twilight Sparkle had arrived to watch, but as usual she was reading her guidebook. "Listen, Rainbow, it says here that the arena was—"

"That's great, Twilight," interrupted Rainbow Dash, "but we're trying to focus on our flying. The race is only a day away."

"We've still got a lot of work to do," added Fluttershy.

"Oops, sorry!" Twilight replied. "Perhaps I'll write a postcard to Spike instead."

Dear Spike,

I spent the day at the Rainbow Falls arena watching Rainbow Dash and the Ponyville Flyers practise for the qualifying race. It was so exciting! The arena is enormous, and it's entirely covered in shimmering grass in perfect condition. Rainbow Dash and Fluttershy have been practising so hard, I hope they will succeed in qualifying for the Games! The Wonderbolts are really good too. I'll write to let you know how the qualifying race goes later!

Your best friend,
Twilight

Twilight had just finished her postcard, when she heard a cry from in the air. One of the Wonderbolts flying team had hurt his wing! "Are you OK?" asked Rainbow Dash, rushing over.

The injury looked serious. "You need to go to hospital," advised Twilight Sparkle. "You're not fit to fly."

Soon a stretcher arrived to take Soarin, the injured pony, to hospital. "We'll come with you to cheer you up," said Pinkie Pie. "No one can be miserable when I'm around!"

Soon Soarin was tucked into bed. "Thank you for your kindness," he told the pony friends. "I just hope my wing is better in time for the competition tomorrow."

"I know it will be," Twilight reassured him. "My guidebook says that Rainbow Falls Hospital is the best in the whole of Equestria. You're definitely in good hooves here . . ."

Finally it was the day of the competition. The Rainbow Falls arena was full of ponies. The cheerleaders were already cheering for their teams – and loudest of all was Pinkie Pie. "Go, Ponyville!" she yelled.

Twilight had even managed to leave her guidebook at the hotel. "This is far more exciting than any book," she told Rarity. "I can't wait to see Rainbow Dash and the Ponyville Flyers in action!"

"I'm so glad Soarin's wing is better so he can compete with the Wonderbolts," added Rarity.

Dear Spike,

Brilliant news . . . Ponyville has qualified for the Equestria Games! Rainbow Dash was amazing. She soared through the arena, past the obstacles and raced straight on to the winner's platform. I'm so proud of her! Fluttershy and Bulk Biceps were great too and didn't drop the horseshoe once!

I can't wait to see you and tell you more about the competition. But first I'm off to celebrate with the team!

Hugs,
Twilight

At last Twilight and her friends arrived back in Ponyville. It was great to be home.

Twilight gave Spike the biggest hug. "Thanks for your postcards," he told her. "I almost felt like I was there in Rainbow Falls with you!"

"It'll be the Equestria Games soon," said Twilight. "And this time we'll all go!"

Dear citizens of Ponyville,

It is my great honour to announce that the Ponyville Flyers have qualified to compete in the Equestria Games aerial relay competition. We are all so proud of Rainbow Dash and her team, and we can't wait to see them take part in the Games to be held in the Crystal Empire. Please join us for a celebration in the town square tomorrow at four o'clock!

With much pride,
Your Ponyville mayor